THE GREEN MONSTER

adapted by Sónia Murphy
based on the original teleplay by Michael Ryan
illustrated by Chris George

Ready-to-Read

Simon Spotlight

New York   London   Toronto   Sydney

SIMON SPOTLIGHT
An imprint of Simon & Schuster Children's Publishing Division
1230 Avenue of the Americas, New York, New York 10020
© 2004 Mirage Studios, Inc. *Teenage Mutant Ninja Turtles*™
is a trademark of Mirage Studios, Inc. All rights reserved.

Manufactured in the United States of America

First Edition

2 4 6 8 10 9 7 5 3 1

Library of Congress Cataloging-in-Publication Data
Murphy, Sonia.
The green monster / adapted by Sonia Murphy ; based on the original teleplay by Michael
Ryan ; illustrated by Chris George.— 1st ed.
p. cm. — (Ready-to-read)
Summary: Casey helps Michaelangelo and Donatello keep a nosey television monster-hunter
from revealing their existence.
ISBN 0-689-86902-9 (pbk.)
[1. Turtles—Fiction. 2. Heroes—Fiction. 3. Monsters—Fiction.] I. George, Chris, 1977- ill.
II. Title. III. Series.
PZ7.M9562 Gr 2004
[E]—dc22
2003018336

Doctor Finn, who hunts monsters, was taping another episode of *The Monster Hunter.*
"Today I am hunting the Green Man of the woods," she said.

Suddenly Casey Jones ran out
from his hiding place.
"Stop the camera!" he yelled.
Doctor Finn asked Casey, "What can
you tell our viewers about
the Green Man of the woods?"

"Uh, look, lady, you have to go.
There is nothing in those woods
except trees," Casey said.
"You are wrong!" exclaimed
Doctor Finn.
"I have proof on this tape!"

Doctor Finn played the tape and
Casey saw his friend Michelangelo
on the screen.

"What do you have to say now?"
asked Doctor Finn.

"I can't see anything," Casey lied.

"Now, hit the highway!"

Meanwhile around the corner
Donatello and Michelangelo were
watching them.
"Uh-oh, that's me on the tape,"
said Michelangelo.
"We have to get that tape!"
exclaimed Donatello.
"Doctor Finn is hunting you!"

"Let's get the tape from her truck!"
said Michelangelo.

"Good idea," said Donatello.
"If she plays that tape on TV,
we could all be in danger."
8

"I don't know, Mikey. This could be a trap," Donatello warned.

But it was too late!
The doors shut and locked.
"We are trapped!" Donatello yelled.
He grabbed a pipe from the wall
and banged on the truck doors.

Finally the doors opened!
Donatello and Michelangelo
jumped out.
"Let's get outta here!"
yelled Donatello.

Back home Donatello, Michelangelo,
and Casey tried to think of a way
to get rid of Doctor Finn.
"I know!" exclaimed Donatello.
"We can pretend to be monsters
and scare Doctor Finn away!"
Michelangelo and Casey agreed.

Casey, Donatello, and Michelangelo covered their bodies with mud, branches, and leaves. They really looked like monsters! Now they were ready to scare Doctor Finn!

The three friends went into
the woods. Casey started howling.
When Doctor Finn spotted him,
she fired her net-gun.
"I've got a monster!" she yelled
to Parker.

Doctor Finn and Parker went to
get their truck.
"Get me out of here!" called Casey.
Michelangelo helped him
out of the net.

Just then they heard a howl—
right next to them!
"It's the real Green Man!"
said Donatello.
They watched as the monster
sniffed at Michelangelo's belt.
"He wants my pistachio nuts!"
said Michelangelo. "Here boy!"

Just then they saw the headlights
of a truck coming toward them.
The Green Man ran off scared.
"It's Doctor Finn! We can't let her
get the Green Man!" Mikey shouted.
"We have to save him!"

"Look, they're forcing the Green Man into the truck! Casey and I will take care of Parker and free the monster while you keep Doctor Finn busy," Donatello told Michelangelo. "Sure thing," Michelangelo replied.

Away from the truck Michelangelo
let out a howl.

Doctor Finn hurried toward the noise.
But she tripped when Michelangelo
stuck his leg out.

"Parker? There is another monster
out here!" Doctor Finn shouted.

As Doctor Finn was talking to
Parker, Michelangelo quickly ran to
the truck and grabbed the tape.
Then he decided to give
Doctor Finn one last scare.

Doctor Finn slowly got to her feet and looked around for the monster. "Boo," said Michelangelo, hanging from a tree behind her. "Ahhhh!" yelled Doctor Finn, running away.

Michelangelo was still laughing
when he jumped down from the tree.
"Waaagh!" he shouted.
"It's only me," said Donatello.
"But where is the Green Man?"
Michelangelo asked.
"All taken care of," replied Donatello.

The next morning Parker had bad
news for Doctor Finn.
"Doctor Finn, the tape is gone!"
he said.
"How?" she asked.

Then she remembered
the Green Man she had caught.
"Wait," said Doctor Finn, "I do not
need the tape. I have a live monster
right here in the truck!"

Later that day Doctor Finn faced
a crowd of reporters.
"Today, I, Doctor Abigail Finn,
have captured a real monster.
I give you the famous Green Man!"
she said.

Parker opened the truck door.

"Help! Save me from that crazy lady!"
yelled Casey.

The reporters started to laugh.

"No!" Doctor Finn shouted.

"How can this be? My monster!
My TV show!"

Facing the reporters, Casey said,
"Can you guys believe this?
She chased me through
the woods all night long!
She should be locked up!"

Back in the woods Michelangelo
and Donatello watched as
Doctor Finn got into her truck.
"But where is the real
Green Man?" Michelangelo
asked.

Donatello pointed to the woods.
There was the Green Man
with two green babies!
Michelangelo and Donatello smiled.

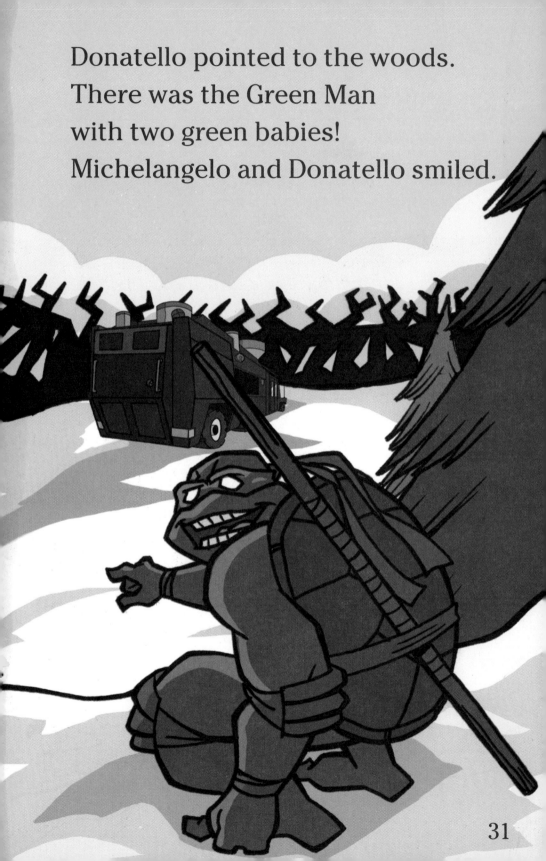

"Just for the record the Green Man
is a she! A mother!" Donatello said.